Out-of-this-world Events

KELL, the ALIEN

THE ALIENS, INC. SERIES
KELL, the ALIEN

By Darcy Pattison

pictures by
Rich Davis

MIMS HOUSE / LITTLE ROCK, AR

Mims House
1309 S. Broadway
Little Rock, AR 72202

www.mimshouse.com.com

Publisher's Note: This is a work of fiction. Names, characters, places, and incidents are a product of the author's imagination. Locales and public names are sometimes used for atmospheric purposes. Any resemblance to actual people, living or dead, or to businesses, companies, events, institutions, or locales is completely coincidental.

Book design © 2013 by BookDesignTemplates.com

Kell, the Alien/ Darcy Pattison — First Edition
Library of Congress Control Number: 2014904869
Paperback ISBN 978-1-62944-021-7
Library Paperback ISBN 978-1497316133
Hardcover ISBN 978-1-62944-020-0
Ebook ISBN 978-1-62944-022-4
Lexile 510L
Printed in the United States of America

For Haileigh

CHAPTER

"Well, did you know my birthday party is next month?" Bree Hendricks said to me. She swiped a splash of blue with her paintbrush. "Do you like my bowl?"

Mrs. Crux, the art teacher had put a blue bowl of fruit on each table and said, "Paint this."

I needed red for the strawberries. But the lid of the red paint jar was stuck.

Bree said, "My nine-year-old birthday party will be special. I want an Alien Party."

"Oh." I don't have to say much with Bree, which is nice.

The paint jar was narrow. I tried to bite the lid to open it. Still stuck.

Bree nodded. "Our principal, Mrs. Lynx doesn't like aliens, but I do. Aliens are so weird that they are magnificent. Wouldn't you like to be an alien? You could fly around Jupiter or something."

"Yes, Jupiter is magnificent." I turned the red paint jar upside down and shook it. Then I tried HARD to open it. Stuck.

Bree smeared yellow for lemons. "How do you know Jupiter is magnificent? You're not an alien."

Bree was wrong.

Jupiter is the fifth planet in this solar system, and it's huge. My family spent a week flying around it. We took pictures and measured scientific stuff. Until Dad leaked his *dovitch*. *Dovitch* is like space-coffee, and Dad drank it every morning. Except one morning, he left the cup open, and the *dovitch* floated out and onto the ship's control panel. Mom says that Dad is forgetful, which he is. But here

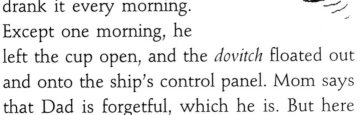

are the facts. Dad's *dovitch* bubbled out, our spaceship went crazy, and then we crash landed on Earth. We hid for a year to figure things out, but we finally sold our spaceship and bought a house. And here I am, my first week in an Earthling school.

But I can't tell Bree all of that.

Now she was painting orange in a big circle.

I took a deep breath, held the jar to my chest and twisted the lid. Come on, open up. Suddenly, it gave way, and the lid went one way and the jar the other. Paint flew across  my paper, across the table. One paint glob floated straight for Aja Dalal, straight for his head, straight for—oh! Right in his ear.

Aja's dark eyes went wide with shock. Kids looked up, groaned—and turned away. Oh, I was the alien here: that was clear.

Mrs. Crux looked up from Freddy's painting with a smile. "Again, mate?" She talks different because she is from a place called Australia. I wonder if she feels like an alien sometimes, too. From her desk, she handed me an instant camera.

I snapped pictures of the table and of Aja's ear. I thumbtacked the pictures to the Accidental Art bulletin board. In just one week, this was my seventh Accidental Art. The rest of the class had zero Accidental Arts.

Later, when Aja and everything else was cleaned up, I sat at the art table with Bree again. It was too late to start a new painting.

Bree dotted brown on her yellow banana and talked about her party again. "Mom will pay somebody to do an Alien Party."

Now I really listened. My mom and dad didn't have jobs, yet. "How much will she pay?"

"Enough so it will be a special party," Bree said.

I thought about that.

WHO? Bree and her friends.

WHAT? An alien birthday party.

WHEN? On Bree's birthday next month.

WHERE? I didn't know.

"Where will you have the party?" I asked.

"Is my back yard big enough for an alien space ship to land there?"

She lived next door to me. "Oh, yes," I said. Back on Bix, there were spaceships large enough to fill up three of Earth's football fields. There were spaceships large enough to carry a dozen Earthling blue whales, the largest animals on Earth. But my family's spaceship was so small that it made a school bus look like a mansion.

I was confused, though. "Where will you get a space ship?"

"You know. A blow-up space ship," she said. "Like a balloon."

"Oh." I didn't know what she meant. I had to put that on my Look Up Later List.

LOOK UP LATER LIST
1. Chewing gum
2. Fingernail clippers
3. Blow-up space ship, balloon

I thought some more. Who? What? When? Where?

WHY? To make Bree happy on her birthday.

HOW? I asked, "How do you do an Alien Party?"

Using a small brush, Bree dotted pink around the edge of her paper. There was nothing pink in the bowl of fruits. Bree just liked pink, like her pink fingernails. "Oh, you know," she said. "Alien music. Alien games. Alien space ships. Alien cake."

I started to get excited. A Bix party on Earth could be fun.

"Your Mom can't do those alien things?" I asked.

"I know—lawyers are aliens. But my mom is just too busy." Then Bree held up her picture. "Do you like it?"

Buzz! Buzz!

An Earthling bug! Bix has no bugs. But there are more bugs on Earth than any other kind of creature. And they all bite. Or sting. I hate all Earthling bugs.

And that black bug was right over out table. I ducked, but it dove at me. It was going to sting me!

I slapped at the bug.

I hit it!

And I knocked it straight into Bree's painting.

It stuck.

There it was. Right there on the yellow banana. It was a huge brown spot.

Oh! I ruined her painting.

Bree called, "Mrs. Crux."

Bree was mad, now, I thought.

Mrs. Crux came over, "What's up, mate?"

"See the fly on the banana?" Bree held up her painting for everyone to see. "My first Accidental Art!"

Kids clapped, and Mrs. Crux thumbtacked Bree's painting to the Accidental Art bulletin board.

Bree fist-bumped me. "We are the best Accidental Artists in third grade."

Other kids fist-bumped Bree. And me. And I was flying high—my first Earthling friend.

Then this idea bubbled up in me. "I can do your Alien Party, if your mom pays me." I added, "Of course, my mom and dad will help."

Bree turned and smiled at me. Her eyes are blue like the Earth sky. When she smiled, it

was like the Earth's sun was shining inside me.

That surprised me a lot, and it was a nice surprise. Of course, I wouldn't tell anyone else. Earthling boys don't talk to Earthling girls. I don't think they like each other.

"Really?" Bree said. "You can do it? You will do a magnificent party." She added, "Oh, thanks to your parents, too."

I grinned. My parents would help. But really, what on Earth did they know how to do?

But then, I frowned. Bree didn't know she was looking at an alien from Bix. Sure, I can see in the dark, and I shed my skin once a month and other things like that. But I look Earthling. Would Bree be friends with an alien?

The bell rang, time for homeroom.

Bree waved at the paintings. "Which do you like best?"

I really liked Aja's Ear best. But I told Bree, "The Fruit Fly."

"Thanks." Bree punched my arm and then skipped out of the room.

Wait. Why did she hit me? Earthling girls are strange.

CHAPTER

"**M**om, Dad! I'm home," I called.

The house smelled green. Mom was at her plant research again.

"OUCH!" From outside somewhere, Dad yelled.

I rushed out the back door. "What happened?"

Dad held his left foot with both hands and jumped around on his right foot. "I dropped the hammer." It lay beside a pile of boards.

That's my Dad. He does astro-physics, but he can't hold onto a hammer.

"I'm glad you're home," Dad said. "You can help."

"What are we building?" I asked.

"A tree house," Dad said.

When we crash landed, we sold our broken space ship to the Weirdest Tales Museum. It took us a year to buy a house because on Bix, we live in tree houses. Now, I counted. There were eleven trees in the back yard. So that's why Dad agreed to buy this house.

"Does Mom know?"

"She will."

"Do we have enough money to build tree houses?" I asked.

Dad's gray eyes twinkled. "Well, after buying our house, we are almost out of money. But we have enough to start a tree house."

I nodded, then said, "I have to tell you about school today. First, I have to tell you something else—Earthlings are born, not hatched."

"I know."

"And you didn't tell me?"

I helped carry wood to the biggest tree. While we worked, I explained about birthday parties, how they are joyful.

We put the silver ladder against the tree. Dad carried the wood up the ladder and stuck it in the crook of a branch. Heaving wood up a tree is hard work. We don't do telekinesis much here because it would scare Earthlings that we can move things with our minds. But here, we used just a tiny bit of telekinesis to make the wood feel lighter.

I explained about Bree's birthday and how she wanted an Alien Party. And how I said I would do it.

Dad said, "No."

Which made me mad. Bree was my first Earthling friend, even if she was a rich girl and spoiled like a Princess, like Freddy and Aja said. I was going to do her party.

About then, I smelled something. Mom was home and was cooking and—Surprise!—it actually smelled good.

Dad was fast building that tree house now. I sat beside him and handed him nails. With every nail, Dad had a reason not to do the party.

"We don't know anything about birthdays."

Bang! Bang! Ouch! He sucked his banged thumb.

"We don't know what Earthlings think aliens are like," Dad said.

Bang! Bang! Ouch! He sucked his first finger.

"You put lots of Earthling children together, and they are unpredictable," Dad said.

Bang! Bang! Ouch!

Hey! That was my hand! Now, I sucked my thumb.

And the floor of the tree house was already done.

Then I smelled something not so nice. My Mom doesn't smell good. Well, she smells good. But her nose doesn't work good and tell her about Earthling smells.

"Mom!" I yelled. "Is supper burning?"

Sure enough, a minute later, Mom stomped out with a smoking pan. She scraped the burned food into the trash can. Again. Then Mom looked around.

Dad held still.

But I called, "Hi, Mom."

Now, Mom tilted her head and frowned. "John, what are you doing?"

"Now, Jane. We can talk about this later."

No one can say our Bix names, so we use easy Earthling names. My name is part of a word on a cereal box: Kell-oggs. Kell Smith is my name.

"We will talk later," Mom promised. "But right now, it's time to eat."

The kitchen table had blue plates and blue glasses. On my plate was a surprise. Carrots and lettuce. What was Mom thinking? I needed FOOD!

Just then, the doorbell rang. I raced to the door and brought Bree's Mom back to the kitchen.

"I just got out of court, but Bob is grilling hamburgers," Mrs. Hendricks said. "It's our chef's night off. Would you like to join us?"

"Yes!" Dad and I said at the same time.

"Thank you!" Mom and I said at the same time.

So, we ate magnificent burgers with the Hendricks. We ate on their back deck under the eighteen trees in their back yard.

After eating—and eating—Mrs. Hendricks said, "Jane, my Bree says you know how to do birthday parties."

"Oh, yes." Mom was completely confused. Her blue-grey eyes were too shiny, like aluminum foil.

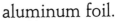

"Bree wants an alien birthday party," Mrs. Hendricks said.

"Sounds fun," Dad said.

"Mrs. Lynx, the principal, doesn't like aliens—she's a UFO chaser. But we think it will be fun," Mrs. Hendricks said. "How much?"

Bree added, "You name a price."

Dad touched Mom's arm, and she clutched at his hand.

"Kell told me about the party," Dad said. "But we didn't discuss—money?"

Mrs. Hendricks said, "We can work out a budget. I know that Bree wants a blow-up space ship."

Dad's eyes got giant-sized. "She wants to blow up a space ship?"

"You know," Mrs. Hendricks said. "A bounce house."

"Oh, I see," Mom said. But of course she didn't see or understand.

My head was spinning. Now I needed an Alien Party List, not just a Look Up Later List.

ALIEN PARTY LIST

1. What is a budget?

2. Where do you find a blow-up balloon, bounce house, or spaceship thingy?

Dad said, "We'll get back to you on a price. But this party will be as easy as flying from star to star."

Mrs. Hendricks laughed. "Nice alien joke."

Could I do a birthday party? No. This was a bad idea. But—money!

Bree whirled around and around. "Hurrah!"

When she stopped, she was facing our yard. "Mr. Smith, what are you building?"

Mom said, "John is building a tree house. He's good at starting things."

"I'm going to sleep up there tonight," Dad said.

Mom and I glared at him. It wasn't fair that he got to sleep in a tree house and we

☆ 24 ☆

had to sleep in the 100-year old Earthling house.

"Wow, a treehouse! I want a tree castle," Bree said. "But if you sleep outside, will bugs bite you?"

And then, I was glad I wasn't going to sleep in Dad's tree house.

Dad frowned, "I don't know. But I'm going to do it any-way."

Later, I would have to explain everything to Mom and Dad and we would have to talk about money. But for now, we just visited. Mom and Mr. Hendricks talked about recipes. Dad and Mrs. Hendricks talked about Earth trees and tree houses.

Later, when the stars came out, Bree showed me all about an Earthling bug named the firefly. She wasn't even scared of those bugs.

Earthling girls are strangely brave.

CHAPTER

The next day, right before lunch, my class went from homeroom to music class.

Mr. Vega, the music teacher, said, "Today, we will start practicing for a Parent's Night concert. Mrs. Lynx is here today to help choose a soloist."

Mrs. Lynx, the principal, sat on a stool beside the piano.

Mr. Vega said, "Who would like to try out for a solo?"

Beside me, Bree raised her hand.

I like to lie on my bed and sing Bix music to the stars and constellations and galaxies out my window. On Bix, Dad and I often sang duets. So I raised my hand, too.

It made me look at my wrist.

I shed my skin yesterday, and there was still one patch with old skin. I pulled my hand down and peeled off the skin and stuck it in my pocket.

Had Bree seen? Or Mrs. Lynx? Or anyone else?

No one said anything or looked at me funny.

Mr. Vega said, "Bree, Kell and Cherry. Come up, and we'll see what you can do."

Bree smiled at me. "I'll get to do the solo, of course."

But I wanted to do it, too. I followed Bree to the front to stand by the tall, red piano.

Mr. Vega said, "Kell, could you sing first, please?"

I started singing and let me tell you, I can hit a note. I stay on the right notes all the time.

My country t'is of thee
Sweet land of liberty
Of Thee I sing.
Land where my fathers died
Land of the Pilgrim's pride
From every mountain side
Let freedom ring.

Of course, my grandfathers didn't die on Earth. They died on Bix. And I didn't know what Pilgrims were. But I could add Pilgrims to my Look Up Later List.

"Kell, I must say, your voice is out of this world," said Mrs. Lynx. Then she used her loud voice to tell me to sing soft. That means, she yelled at me, "Please, sing softer!"

Uh-oh. Mrs. Lynx, the UFO-Chaser, was on my tail. So I just stopped singing.

Mr. Vega frowned. "Thanks, Kell.

Let's hear Bree and Cherry try it."

While Cherry and Bree sang, I looked at the top of the piano. Mr. Vega had statues of famous musicians like Mozart and Bach.

I always felt sorry for really good Earthling musicians. None of them had arms or legs.

Mrs. Lynx frowned at me, so I turned back to the singing.

Cherry's voice bounced around. She sang loud and soft, but she could not stay on the right notes.

Bree sang the notes, and she did loud and soft, too.

Mrs. Lynx smiled, "Bree, you can sing the solo."

Then Bree smiled, and that smile made the Earth's sun shine inside me again. Except a black thundercloud came out and covered the sun. Because I wanted to sing that solo.

That Bree. She stole the solo away from me. I

was better than Cherry. I was better than Bree.

Walking out to lunch, Mrs. Lynx stopped me and bent to stare straight into my eyes. "Do you have a cold or something?"

Her eyes were dark blue, almost navy. What would she do if she found out I was an alien? My family didn't get Earthling colds. But it was an easy way to explain my loud singing. "Yes, ma'am. I just got over a cold."

She frowned, but walked off, shaking her head.

In the lunchroom, I told Bree, "That song is still running around in my head."

"That must mean there's nothing in your head to get in its way. Ha." Bree smiled to show that was a joke.

I frowned at my lunch plate. It was green beans, meat loaf and chocolate 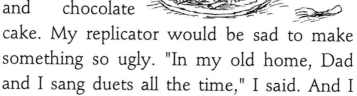 cake. My replicator would be sad to make something so ugly. "In my old home, Dad and I sang duets all the time," I said. And I ached suddenly for the red skies of Bix. Would we ever get home?

Bree said, "'My Country T'is of Thee' is historical. Everyone has to learn it."

"Well, it's a dumb song," I said.

Now Bree looked mad. "That is not a fact." She ate a quick bite of her cake, then frowned and pushed it away. She never liked the school food, but her mother wouldn't let her bring their chef's food to school.

Just then, I heard a BUZZ. Quick, I looked around. It was another flying bug.

"What is it? Will it sting?" I could barely breathe.

"A wasp. Yes, it stings!"

It was flying my way.

Buzz. Buzz. Closer.

Buzz. Closer.

I stood up fast. And there went my lunch tray. It went up and up and sent chocolate cake and green beans and meat loaf flying.

"Oh!" Bree yelled, and kids yelled, and everything in the lunchroom was loud.

Quick, I took off my shoe and knocked that wasp to the ground and then hit it with the shoe. That wasp was dead.

Dead.

Dead.

Dead.

I hate all Earthling bugs!

And everything in the lunchroom was quiet.

Quiet.

Quiet.

Quiet.

OK, I thought, it is possible to put lots of kids in a small room and get them to be quiet.

Then, I sat down hard. And everyone started talking again.

A chunk of cake fell off of Bree's hair. Plop! Right into her napkin. She whispered, "That was magnificent." Then, she giggled.

I put on my shoe and watched her clean the cake out of her hair with her napkin. Bree knew just what to say to make things OK. How did she do that?

Earthling girls are funny. And nice.

CHAPTER

4

The next day, after school, Mom picked up Bree and me. We drove to a costume and party shop. It was time to get to work on the Alien party.

Mom, Bree and I walked into a dim, cluttered room. Clothes racks held shiny costumes, while masks covered every wall. A man was behind a counter with his back to us.

Mom said, "Excuse me, sir."

The man turned and—a skeleton! Bree yelped. I grabbed Mom's arm.

The man pulled up his glow-in-the-dark mask, and it perched on top of his head. "My name is Mr. Jasper. Can I help you?"

Mom chuckled, "Good joke." She peeled my fingers off her arm and asked, "Do you have alien costumes?"

Mr. Jasper pointed to a room in the back. "Everything in there is alien."

In the alien room, Bree pulled a shiny green outfit off a rack and grabbed a mask from the wall. She ducked into a changing room. When she came out, her body was a skinny stalk and the mask was twice as big as her head. She looked like a broccoli with shiny eyes.

Bree stood in front of a mirror. "I'm an alien."

"Not really," I said.

Bree got serious. "Scientists have pictures of real aliens, and this is what they look like."

What on Earth did I know? Maybe some alien somewhere looked like that. But I had never met that kind of alien. And I've been around the universe.

Even Mom hated that green costume. "I don't think scientists have the right pictures."

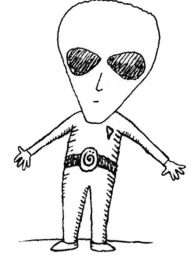

Bree twirled, watching herself in the mirror. "We could rent different costumes and play dress-up."

"No." I had seen her play dress-up with pink tutus. I said, "Girls play dress up, but not boys."

The skeleton popped its head into the room. It said, "You want to see the newest thing in space games? Come, look."

In another back room, Bree held up a silver suit. Fat silver arms and legs were connected to a fat ball in the middle. "It looks weird."

"Let's try it," I said.

But Bree dropped the suit and spun around to a rack. "Alien sunglasses! We have to get these."

We both tried on the alien sunglasses and stood in front of a mirror.

"You know the difference between you and me?" I asked. "I make these glasses look good."

Bree just rolled her eyes at my joke.

"OK," Mom said, "we'll get alien sunglasses if the budget allows. But come try this space suit game."

So Bree and I climbed into the suits. It was like trying to climb into a sticky balloon. Mom strapped on my safety helmet, which looked like a space suit helmet.

Mr. Jasper helped Bree with her helmet.

I tried to walk, but I couldn't even take a step. I fell over.

Mom pulled me up and grinned, "Come on, act like a spaceman."

Bree and I stood on a red mat, which

represented the space ship. The game had easy rules. You try to knock the other person into outer space. On the mat, I was safe. Off the mat, I lost.

The blow-up suit was so tight that I couldn't bend my knees or elbows. I stumbled toward Bree, who shuffled toward me. The blow-up bellies were so big that we ran into each other. Bump! Splat! I fell again.

Lying flat, I couldn't see her, but I heard Bree giggling.

Mom pulled me up again, and I saw Bree on the  ground, too. We had bumped so hard that we both fell backwards. When Bree stood again, we charged. Bump-Kaboom!

This was way better than playing dress-up. Bree laughed so hard, she snorted a funny noise.

We were both standing up again. I decided it was time to push Bree off the mat and win. I charged. Bree just sidestepped.

And I didn't change direction, didn't stop. I fell forward and landed in outer space.

"Yes! I win!" Bree called.

Mom was cracking up so hard, she could barely get the words out, "We have to get this for the party."

And that meant, I won. No dress up. No pink tutus. It was a good start to planning the Alien Party.

"Yes. Let's do it again," Bree said.

But I said, "Not right now."

Because Earthling girls don't need to get used to winning.

CHAPTER

T he next week in music class, Mr. Vega said, "Today, class, we will practice standing on risers for the Parent's Night concert."

Mr. Vega started pointing to kids and telling them where to stand.

The risers are long boards with legs. The risers in front had short legs. The risers in back had long legs. Risers make it easy to see the kids in the back row. Standing on the back row with me, Freddy and I looked eye-to-eye. But Aja was so short, he stared at my shoulder. At last, everyone was in place.

Mr. Vega tapped his stick on the music stand, which meant, "Pay attention."

Freddy's mom, Mrs. Rubin, played the red piano. Her red fingernails danced across the black and white keys.

Bree sang into the microphone, "My Country T'is of Thee." I tried not to listen because it should be me singing the solo. When Bree finished singing, she stepped back in line on the risers.

Just then the music room door opened and Principal Lynx walked in. Her white hair stuck out all over. "Just ignore me," she told Mr. Vega. "I just want to listen to the choir practice." She sat on a chair by the door.

It was time for the choir's great song, "The Star Spangled Banner." I come from the stars, and anything about stars is good even if it's just a song about stars on a flag.

It's really a song about fighting a battle. At dawn, the soldiers looked to see if the flag was still flying. That meant Fort McHenry was still safe. Well, not safe, because they were fighting a war. But the Fort hadn't given up the fight yet.

Mr. Vega tapped his stick on the music stand. He raised his stick, Mrs. Rubin started playing the piano, and we sang:

Oh, say can you see?
By the dawn's early light
What so proudly we hailed
At the twilight's last gleaming?
Whose broad stripes and bright stars—

Mr. Vega gave the stick and his hands a twist. That meant, "Stop singing."

Why did we stop? I was singing that part about stars with emotion.

Mr. Vega said, "Kell, you are singing too loud. Can you PLEASE try to sing softly?"

All the kids groaned at me. Mrs. Rubin frowned, and Principal Lynx glared.

I gulped, swallowing my joy in the song. "Yes, sir."

"The rest of you sing louder," Mr. Vega said. "And sing faster. Aja, you play the tambourine to make a beat everyone can hear. Watch me, and I can help you sing at the right speed."

Mr. Vega tapped his stick and started the song again. This time, I lip-synced, which means I just mouthed the words. With Aja's tambourine, we sang faster. Mr. Vega put down his stick and clapped. "Good job!"

Walking out of music class, Mrs. Rubin stopped me. "Kell, you are supposed to sing, you know."

Mrs. Lynx was watching us. "Yes, Ma'am," I said.

Mrs. Rubin closed the lid of the piano. "You can sing softly. I know you can."

"Yes, Ma'am." I was so angry that I wanted to open that piano and pound on the keys. Instead, I just walked past her.

But at the door, Mrs. Lynx eyed me up and down. My knees went all alien and wobbly with fear. I spun away and staggered down the hall.

"Next time, sing," Principal Lynx called after me. "I'll be watching."

I nodded but didn't turn back.

It rained all afternoon, and I wanted to hum a Bix song to cheer myself up. But I couldn't do it soft enough. So I just sat in home room and stared at the rain.

Principal Lynx's words kept echoing in my head, "I'll be watching you."

After school, Mom and Dad were up in one of the tree houses. Dad kept finding wood by the side of the road that someone wanted to throw away. But they didn't care if someone else took the wood. They just wanted it gone. So Dad had built two more big tree house floors. He planned to make the tree houses look like space ships.

The storm was over, and I climbed up to watch Dad building.

Mom handed Dad a nail and said, "There's only enough money for another week of food. But then they want us to pay for electricity and gas and—"

Dad held the nail to a board. "Mrs. Hendricks paid us half—Ouch!—of the Alien party money. We can use that money—Ouch!—for bills and use the replicator—Ouch!"

Mom took the hammer from Dad. "Let me do it." She hammered one nail, then said, "The replicator barely works on Earth electricity. If it burns out—"

That surprised me. "I thought the replicator worked good."

"I made it work on Earthling electricity," Dad said. "But the replicator can't make something from nothing. It has to have the white cubes to start with. And we are running low on those. I haven't found anything here on Earth that works."

Mom mumbled, "And he's tried almost everything."

So that was why it smelled funny in the kitchen sometimes.

Dad sighed. "You're probably right. We shouldn't use the replicator except for emergencies."

Now I understood why we only had Bix food once a week. I thought Mom was just trying to make us eat Earthling food. My parents were really trying hard to make things work here on Earth.

Then Dad asked, "How was school today?"

"Horrible. I can't sing soft. The principal heard me sing too loud, then caught me not singing at all. She says that she will be watching me."

"Oh, no." Mom put a hand to her mouth.

"But you know how to sing soft and loud," Dad said. "We do it all the time."

I crossed my arms and said, "You try it."

Dad sang a Bix song.

Wow. He sang loud.

Then Mom sang a line, and she was loud.

"I wonder," she said, "Maybe it's the Earth's air."

They sat on the edge of the tree house, dangling their legs and working on the loud-soft problem. Even though Principal Lynx was a UFO-Chaser and she was after me, they looked happy because they had a science problem to work out. And while they worked on the loud-soft problem, they would forget about Principal Lynx.

I thought of Bree singing the solo and wished we could sing it as a duet. But she didn't need a second voice.

Earthling girls sing as sweetly as Bix crooners, the royal birds.

CHAPTER

"Hand in your insect reports, please," said Mrs. Tarries, our homeroom teacher. She has spiky red hair, a black face and skinny black pants. If she had antennae, she would look like a black and red ant. Mrs. Tarries says insects are her favorite animals. Someday I might get used to living on Earth. But I will never, ever like bugs.

Freddy pulled out his neatly stapled papers. Aja grabbed crumpled papers from his backpack.

I raised my hand.

"Yes, Kell?"

"Mrs. Tarries, I forgot my insect report at home. Can I bring it tomorrow?"

Across the aisle, Bree glared at me. But I didn't know why.

Mrs. Tarries stood over my desk and tapped my backpack. "Kell, you know the class rules. You have one day to bring it in. If you forget again, then you get a zero. And you have to see Mrs. Lynx. "

I did not want a zero. And I really did not want to see Mrs. Lynx. I would write the report that night.

At lunchtime, Bree was waiting for me. Her arms were crossed, and her blue eyes were like laser guns. "Did you write your insect report last night?"

"No." I decided to give her a compliment, so she wouldn't be mad. "But thank you for teaching me about fireflies. I have decided to write about fireflies."

In a voice like a TV judge, she said, "You did not tell the truth, the whole truth and nothing but the truth."

the TRUTH, the WHOLE TRUTH, and NOTHING BUT the TRUTH!

Bree's mom is a lawyer, so I know this saying. It's what people in court have to swear about telling the truth. But I'm a liar. I lie every day when I let Bree think I am an Earthling.

Bree said, "You have to tell Mrs. Tarries the truth. You need a zero for today."

"No way! Why would I do that?"

Bree's eyes were wide, and she breathed funny. "To tell the truth."

I couldn't do that. Here on Earth, I had to lie to stay alive. I said, "No."

Bree picked up her orange cafeteria tray. "Then we are not friends."

She marched over to a table of girls and sat beside Mary Lee and Cherry.

Right away, Freddy sat down at my table. "Ugh. Finally, that girl left."

Why don't Earthling boys like Earthling girls? It's so strange.

Then Aja came over and brought Edgar van Dyke in his wheelchair, and the guys started playing food games. First, Freddy packed thirty French fries into his mouth. Then Edgar crammed ten chicken nuggets into his mouth. Aja shoved ten French fries, ten chicken nuggets, and two cookies into his

mouth at the same time and he won.

Really? It was nine French fries because I counted. Was it a lie that Aja said he ate ten French fries? Did a small lie like that matter?

Bree didn't look at me or talk to me again all day. The Earth sun was not shining inside me. It was as dark as midnight in there.

That evening, I was surprised Bree still came over to talk about the party.

She frowned and said, "Well, we still have to figure out the food."

Mom and Dad were in the study working on the loud-soft problem. The study was full of machines and wires and things that didn't work to call home to Bix.

So I took Bree to the dining room and got straight to business. "Look. I'm sorry I lied about the insect report. I have it written now, all about fireflies."

Bree crossed her arms and glared.

"I'll turn in the firefly report tomorrow," I said. "And I'll tell Mrs. Tarries I'm sorry."

Bree said. "You'll tell her the truth, the whole truth, and nothing but the truth?"

I held up a hand and said, "I swear."

Then Bree smiled.

And the sun was shining inside me again! Mrs. Tarries could give me a zero: I didn't care. I would never lie to Bree again.

"You sit here," I said. "I'll bring you some alien things, and you can tell me if you like them for your party."

Bree nodded.

In the kitchen, I used the replicator to make my favorite Bix food, grawlies. The

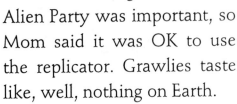

Alien Party was important, so Mom said it was OK to use the replicator. Grawlies taste like, well, nothing on Earth.

Bree frowned at the plate of grawlies. "They look like black French fries."

I ate two of them. "In my part of the galaxy, these are the best."

She popped one into her mouth and chewed. "Hmmm. Sweet. Salty."

I waited for Bree's smile. I waited for her to say grawlies were magnificent.

Instead, Bree shoved back her chair and stuck out her tongue and started waving her hand at her tongue.

Strange, I thought.

She gasped, "Water."

Her face turned red. Worried, I rushed into the kitchen, and she followed. I grabbed a glass, filled it with water, gave it to her, and she drank and drank.

Then she hopped up and down, tears running down her cheeks and gasping, "Make it quit burning."

She drank and drank and drank some more.

Finally, she collapsed on the floor and glared up at me. I squatted beside her, not daring to touch her.

Bree jabbed her finger at me. "That was so spicy hot. You tried to kill me."

What if I had hurt her? My *bligfa* hurt just thinking about it.

Before I could answer, she stopped and pointed. "What is that?"

The replicator.

Uh, oh.

Bree wasn't supposed to be in the kitchen. The replicator is smaller than a stove but larger than a microwave. It does not look like anything in an Earth kitchen.

"That?" I had to think fast. "Dad is an inventor. It's a replicator."

"Like on Star Trek?"

"Yes, but for this replicator to work, you put in these cubes first." I was talking too much, but Bree had to believe Dad was an inventor. I pulled a handful of soft white cubes from a paper bag and put a dish of cubes into the replicator.

Bree said, "Make an apple."

For the replicator to work, it first needs a sample to analyze. Once it makes a kind of food, you can save that food's setting and make it again. I used the English keyboard to type, "Apple."

Whirr. Whirr. Ding.

I opened the replicator and handed Bree an apple.

"Wow." Bree took a bite. "That tastes good."

"Where do you get those cubes?" She nodded at the paper bag and took another bite of her apple.

From Bix, of course. But I said, "From another country." More lies. And I had just promised myself not to lie any more. I felt terrible, but what could I do?

"Oh. Overseas."

Time to change the subject. "You don't like grawlies, but we can try other alien food. What other kind of food do you want at the party?" I asked.

"A birthday cake."

"Birthday cakes aren't alien."

"You have to have birthday cake. Everyone knows that."

"Except an alien," I said.

But I knew I had lost this battle. Because Earthling girls sure are stubborn.

CHAPTER

I have never eaten a birthday cake.

Bree ran home and brought back some of their chef's chocolate cake, her favorite.

Mom and Dad were still in the study working on the loud-soft problem.

"Will the replicator make a cake?" Bree asked.

"I think so." I put a slice of the chef's cake into the replicator and pushed ANALYZE.

Whirr. Whirr.

Crunch.

The replicator said, "Can not analyze."

"Don't worry," I told Bree, "This happens sometimes. It

just means you have to analyze every ingredient by itself. What's in it?"

"Flour, sugar, baking powder."

"We already analyzed those—" I stopped. I almost said, "—those Earth baking ingredients." I had to be careful or Bree would figure out we were aliens.

"Vanilla and chocolate," she said.

"Do you have some of that at your house? Can you go get it and anything else that goes into the cake recipe?"

She was back soon with a small bag. From the bag, she handed me a small jar.

I poured vanilla flavoring into a bowl, set it in the replicator and pushed ANALYZE.

Whirr, whirr, ding.

"Great, it worked."

Just then, Mom called from the study. "Be right back," I said.

Mom had a funny metal thing that she put on my neck and told me to sing. I still sang loud. Shaking her head, she took it off and waved me back to the kitchen.

When I walked back into the kitchen, the replicator was running.

Whirr, whirr, whirr.

It was taking too long. I reached for the replicator door when—Bang!

Bree screamed. I jumped back!

Whirr, whirr, Bang! Smoke spilled from the replicator.

I pulled the electric plug and then banged on the study door and yelled, "Mom! Dad!"

Without waiting for an answer, I pulled Bree out the front door, onto the grass.

"What did you put in the replicator?" I asked Bree.

"Just an egg."

I stared at her in horror. An egg. In our replicator.

Earthlings are born, but Bixsters (what we all ourselves) are hatched. We come from eggs. My family will not eat an egg.

"Do all cakes have eggs?" I demanded.

"Mostly," she said.

Suddenly panicked, I demanded, "What else has eggs in it?"

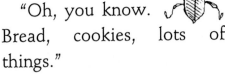

"Oh, you know. Bread, cookies, lots of things."

I wanted to throw up. I had been eating chocolate cake at school every day. I had never felt so much like an alien.

Just then, Mom and Dad came rushing outside. I told them about the replicator accident, and Dad went inside to look. He came back out in a minute and said, "It's OK. No fire."

I frowned. "Did the egg burn up or explode or what?"

Dad said, "Exploded. I threw it away."

Good. I didn't want to see that dead egg.

And I didn't want to do the Alien Party anymore. Everything here on Earth was too hard.

Bree smiled at me, but I couldn't find even the tiniest ray of sunshine. Heavy thunderclouds hung over me. Bree wanted pink dress-up tutus. She didn't like grawlies because they were too spicy. And Earthling cakes were made with eggs! Eggs!

An Alien Party on Earth was impossible. The only way to do it was the Earthling way. I gave up. OK. Bree would get an Earthling Alien Party.

Because Earthling girls deserve Earthling birthday parties.

CHAPTER

N ow it was just one week before Bree's party. Time to print invitations. She wanted cards with a picture of that green alien face, so she got that stupid picture. Inside the card, we invited kids to the party on Friday night.

The next day at school, Bree went up and down the aisles passing out the invitations. But on the other side of the room, Freddy was passing out something, too.

Bree and Freddy looked at each other when they passed. And it started.

Aja held up two invitations. "You're both having birthday parties on Friday?"

Just then, the bell rang and Mrs. Tarries started to call roll.

I remembered thinking about Bree's birthday party the first time I heard about it. Who, What, When, Where and Why? To make Bree happy.

If half of Bree's friends went to Freddy's party, she would not be happy. Freddy's invitation said, "Pizza Party at Pizza Planet." That was not as good as an Alien Party.

At lunch, Freddy sat beside me with his cheese sandwiches. I had an eggless lunch that Mom had packed for me.

Freddy asked, "Are you coming to my party, or Bree's?"

I explained that my parents were doing Bree's party. "I might have to help them."

Freddy shook his head and chomped on his sandwich. He crunched his chips and

my party
is
ruined

snapped a carrot in half. Finally, he said, "My party is ruined because of Bree."

I wanted Freddy to have a Happy Birthday, too. "No," I said, "I'll figure out something."

"Really?"

I handed him a napkin and pointed at the apple pie on his nose. "Yes, I'll figure out something."

But that was a lie.

Walking home after school, Bree worried, "What if no one comes to my party?"

I told Bree the same thing I told Freddy. "Don't worry. I will figure out something."

But that was another lie.

All week, I heard kids talking, "Whose party will you go to?"

By Thursday, I still had no idea how to fix the problem of two parties.

Thursday night was the Parent's Night Concert. The noisy cafeteria was full of parents and kids. The risers and Mrs. Rubin's red piano took up most of the stage.

Just as we walked in, Mrs. Lynx said into the microphone: "Everyone sit. It's almost time to start."

Dad, Mom and I sat at the back of the cafeteria and listened as the kindergarten sang. Then first grade sang. Then second grade sang. Then it was time for third grade.

I walked up to the risers and told Bree, "Good luck on your solo." Really, I wished we were singing a duet, not a solo. But Mom and Dad hadn't solved the problem of why Bixsters can only sing loud on Earth.

Then, it hit me. A duet.

That was the answer.

Bree and Freddy could do their parties together, like singing a duet. After the concert I would talk to Mrs. Hendricks and Mrs. Rubin about a duet party.

Would it work? For the first time in a week, I had some hope.

Mr. Vega stopped me at the bottom of the risers. "Aja is sick," he said. "I want you to play the tambourine."

"OK." I couldn't sing, but maybe I could do a good tambourine beat.

Finally, every third grade kid was in place. The cafeteria was packed, and suddenly all those Earthlings made my *bligfa* hurt. I couldn't look at so many people at once, so I looked up at the ceiling. And there they were. Lots of spider webs.

Quick, I raised my hand.

But Mr. Vega tapped his stick on the music stand. The room was quiet. Mrs. Rubin started playing the red piano, and Bree started to sing.

And a big spider started coming down toward me, hanging on an invisible thread. What if the spider thread broke? That spider might fall right on top of me. I wanted to shout at Mr. Vega to do something about that spider. But Bree was singing.

The spider
dropped closer.
Here's a fact:
some spider
bites make you sick.
I shoved at Freddy
and tried
to side-step
away from
the spider.
Freddy waved
his hand trying to catch his balance, and that
made him lean on Mary Lee, who leaned on
Cherry. That made everyone else fall
sideways, too.

Then that spider dropped right for my
eyes.

I jumped off the back of the risers and
covered my head and waited—for the BITE!

Screams.

The piano stopped.

Then Bree stopped singing.

I looked up.
Kids sprawled all
over the risers.

Mrs. Rubin glared
at me. Mr. Vega glared
at me. Bree glared at me.

Mrs. Lynx, the UFO chaser, glared at me.

I pointed up and said, "Spiders."

There was a chorus of chuckles from the audience.

And I wanted to hide.

Mr. Chamale, the
school custodian, rushed
forward with a huge broom
and swatted away at the
ceiling. He even stood
on the top of the risers
and jumped up and
swatted at spiders.

SWISH!

Finally, Mr. Chamale told Mrs. Lynx, "Spiders all gone." He went back stage with his broom.

I turned to see Mrs. Rubin shaking her head. What if she said no about the duet party?

And then Bree was in front of me. She said one word,

"Magnificent."

That Bree.

She always knew what to say to make things better.

There was no time for more. I scrambled up the risers to my place and Mr. Vega tapped his stick. The music started, and Bree was singing her song again.

And for the first time—I really listened. Before, I was busy being jealous that I wasn't singing the solo.

Wow! She sang it with emotion. Her song made the sun come out and start shining inside me again. And it felt good to let Bree be good at what

Bree was good at.

Maybe Bree was trying to let me be good at what I was good at, too. She was trying to let me do an Alien Party—my way. What if I forgot about all the Earthling ideas that say an Alien Party is supposed to be like this or like that. Could I do a truly Alien Party for her? She was trusting me to do that, wasn't she?

OK, I would try it. Mrs. Lynx, the UFO chaser, might figure out we were aliens, but it didn't matter. Bree was going to get her Alien Party.

Mr. Vega tapped his stick on the stand again. "The Star Spangled Banner" started out too  slow. I beat the tambourine faster, and Mrs. Rubin played faster, and everyone sang faster.

Finally, we finished singing and filed off the risers. I handed the tambourine back to Mr. Vega, and he said, "Nice beat."

Mr. Vega was smiling. Wow!

Then he turned around to help the fourth graders get ready to sing.

I sat beside Dad and waited for the fourth and fifth grades to finish singing. At last, the concert was over.

nice
BEAT

Quick, I found Mrs. Hendricks. "Do you know that Freddy has a party tomorrow, too?" I asked.

"Yes. Too bad. Bree won't have as many people at her party as we hoped."

"What if Bree and Freddy have a party together?" I asked. "Like singing a duet."

"Yes. Of course," she said. "Why didn't we think of that before?"

Now I just had to convince Mrs. Rubin. She was still at the red piano. She closed the lid on the keys and turned.

"Kell? Did you need something?"

I couldn't speak. Mrs. Rubin was mad because I was scared of spiders and messed up the concert.

"Ummm."

"Yes?"

With a shaky voice, I said, "Do you know that Bree has a birthday party tomorrow, too, just like Freddy?"

"Yes. Whose party are you going to?" Her eyes narrowed.

"Ummm."

"Speak up."

So, I spoke up, fast— and loud. "I have an idea. What if Bree and Freddy have a party together? A duet."

Suddenly, Freddy and Bree, Mom and Dad, and Mr. and Mrs. Hendricks were all around us.

Mom said, "Mrs. Rubin, I am Jane Smith, Kell's mom. We hope you will agree to have the parties together."

we've always Liked Duets

A tall man came up and put his arm around Mrs. Rubin.

"This is my husband, Jacob Rubin." She smiled up at him. "Duet? We've always liked duets."

And Freddy nodded his head, too. "Will there be prizes?"

"Of course," Mom said.

Bree skipped around the group and yelled to everyone else, "We are having a duet party. You can all come to both parties, because they are the same party."

Walking out, Mrs. Rubin told Mom, "We will split the costs with the Hendricks. Except can you do a separate birthday cake for Freddy?"

Mom nodded.

"Can I give you a note about what to write on Freddy's cake?" Mrs. Rubin asked.

"Of course," Mom said.

Mrs. Rubin found paper in her purse and wrote something and gave it to Mom.

Walking out, Bree said to me, "Thanks for fixing the party." Then, she punched my arm and skipped after her parents.

Wait. Did she just hit me AGAIN?

When an Earthling girl hits you, does it mean they like you or don't like you?

CHAPTER

The party planning was over. We knew WHO was coming. We knew WHAT: it was an Alien Party. We had fixed the WHEN, so Freddy and Bree could have a duet party. We knew WHERE to have the party. We knew HOW, with games, cakes, and alien sunglasses. Tonight was the night.

All day, Mom and Dad cleaned and cooked and decorated. They worked and worked and worked. When I got home from school, I helped set up the food table.

Just at 6 p.m., Mary Lee and her Dad walked toward my back yard fence.

She said, "My Dad wants to stay and watch a while. Is that OK?"

"Sure," I said.

Aja and Freddy came up behind them. And I saw other kids coming.

"Welcome! And Happy Birthday, Freddy." From a cardboard box, I handed each person a pair of lime-green alien sunglasses.

Bree came up, too, and she wore an alien costume. Let me tell you, she looked like—a broccoli.

I opened the gate to my back yard to let them in. Even I stared in awe. I knew it was just green Christmas lights, a bounce house, eleven trees, some tree houses and some wind chimes. But it was no longer just a back yard.

An eerie green glow swirled across a peculiar landscape. Straight ahead shimmered a flying saucer, and everywhere fireflies flickered. Long, inky shadows marked the pillars of a spaceport, and glowing overhead, a spaceship was docked at each pillar. From above came an unearthly music, deep melodic tones mixed with a sweet tinkling. The stars were singing!

Freddy stepped forward and then spun to stare with wide eyes. "Wow, it even feels alien to walk."

"Mom just grows thick grass," I said. But my grin widened because Dad had installed an anti-gravity machine. As soon as a person stepped into the backyard, they weighed a tiny bit less than normal. Just walking felt alien.

Freddy told Aja, "Let's try the flying saucer first." They sprang away toward the bounce house.

Mary Lee and Bree bounded over to the food table.

Everything was going great, I thought. Bree and Freddy were happy. What could go wrong now?

And then Principal Lynx walked up. She leaned down until her face was level with mine and whispered, "Tonight, I will catch an alien."

Startled, I said, "I feel safer already."

She smiled at that and took the alien sunglasses from my hands and slipped them on. Lime green glasses, white hair—she looked very alien to me. She stalked into the party.

My *bligfa* hurt so bad. Mom and Dad and I had already talked about Principal Lynx looking for clues to aliens. We couldn't stop her, Dad said, so we just had to keep our secrets.

I let out a big sigh. The party had started, and everyone had come. Even Mrs. Tarries, Mr. Vega, and Mrs. Crux were eating star-shaped sugar cookies.

Now, Freddy was dressed up in one of the blow-up space suits. When he got bumped off the mat and into outer space, Mom pulled him up. He got a prize for winning three times in a row. It was a framed picture of an alien.

He waddled over to me and asked, "Do aliens pee in their space suits?"

"No," I said.

"Then you better help me get this off fast," he said. He toppled over to the ground, and I tugged off the suit. A minute later, he dashed into the house to find the bathroom.

And I told Mom, "I'm itching. All over."

"Not now!" Mom said.

"Tonight," I said.

"After the presents, go up to your room and take care of it," she said. "I'll come and check on you later."

I nodded.

From the deck, Dad called, "Time for cake and presents."

He went into the kitchen to get the cake, and I hurried to help.

Alone in the kitchen, Dad told me, "You know, a crowd of Earthling children isn't so bad. This is fun."

I grinned and propped the kitchen door open. Dad held Freddy's coconut cake in both hands and stepped outside. And tripped.

He fell slowly, arms held straight out, trying to protect the cake. I couldn't help it, I used a tiny bit of telekinesis to hold him up. Not much. Just enough to keep Dad from hurting himself. His hands still hit first, and he still skidded across the deck. His face still landed right in the middle of the cake.

Dad sat up, covered with cake and frosting.

And the kids just cracked up.

Principal Lynx shoved to the front of the crowd. "Did you see that?" she demanded. "He didn't really fall. Someone or something held him up."

She was really good: she saw everything! Fortunately, everyone ignored Mrs.Lynx. Mostly, kids were still laughing as Dad scraped icing from his eyes.

Just then, Freddy came out the kitchen door and saw the broken cake. He bent and grabbed a chunk of cake with his bare hands. He threw the cake at Bree.

She squealed in shock.

Oh, that Freddy!

Bree needed a towel to clean up. But I was frozen.

Meanwhile, Mrs. Lynx backed away from the broken cake and Freddy and Bree.

Bree reached up and swiped the icing off her eyebrow. "OK, Freddy. You asked for it."

She grabbed a chunk of cake with her bare hands and threw it at Freddy.

Mrs. Hendricks's eyes were wide. She called, "A cake fight!"

Only Earthlings would think a birthday cake fight was fun.

CHAPTER

I stared as cake flew everywhere. Bree's hair was covered with white. She saw me watching and threw a chunk of cake at me. I turned away, but the cake smacked right into my ear. Bree just smiled.

And right there, in the middle of the birthday cake fight, the Earth's sun shone straight through me and filled me up. And  that still surprises me a lot when that it happens.

For a while, kids threw cake everywhere. What a magnificent mess!

When Mom and Dad realized that no one was mad, they just stood back and watched. When the cake was gone, they helped hose off sticky hair and dry off clothes. Then they hosed off the deck.

Quick, I ran to the kitchen to make a new cake in the replicator. But the bag of white cubes was empty. I searched, but there were none anywhere in the cabinets.

Mom came in and said, "We are all out of cubes. The replicator won't work."

And it really hit me. We were on our own here on Earth.

"Don't worry," Mom said. She had made a large, eggless chocolate cake for Bree and an extra, eggless cake—just in case kids ate a lot. Quickly, she wrote words with icing on the second cake for Freddy.

After everyone was cleaned up, Mom and I brought out the two new cakes—slow and careful—and everyone sang, "Happy birthday!"

Bree pointed at her cake and asked, "What does that mean?"

Bree's cake said: "Happy Breeday!"

Mom said, "Isn't that right? Today is the day of your birth. It is Bree's Day."

Bree grinned. "I guess it is Bree's Day."

Then, Freddy pointed at the other cake. "What does that mean?"

Written on the cake was this:

"Happy Birthday.
Then Underneath,
We love you son,
Mom and Dad."

Everyone laughed.

Frowning, Mom pulled out a paper from her jeans pocket. "That's what your Mom said to write."

"That's funny," Freddy said.

Later, I would explain to Mom that it was funny because she was supposed to leave out the instructions, "Then Underneath."

The full moon had risen during the party, and now it shone a golden light on our deck.

Bree and Freddy blew out all nine plus nine candles on the birthday cakes.

Then, I worried. Would they like eggless chocolate cake?

Bree took the first bite. With her mouth full, she tried to talk, "Mmss."

But I knew what she meant: Magnificent.

For a few minutes everyone ate cake. Except Mrs. Lynx. She just walked around and bent to look at kids' faces. I could not relax till this party was over and she was gone.

Just then Mary Lee's Dad came over to talk to Mom and Dad. "I'm Chief Glendale, the Chief of Police."

"Oh," Dad said.

I didn't know Mary Lee's dad was a policeman. Were we in trouble?

Mrs. Lynx came over to listen.

"This is such a great party," Chief Glendale said. "Do you do other events? The Friends of Police need someone to organize a school parade. We have a small budget to pay you."

Mrs. Hendricks overheard that and turned around. "I think I have something to say about that."

I held my breath. This was it.

"I can't believe that cake fight," Mrs. Hendricks said.

I groaned.

She went on, "My twelve-year-old party had a cake fight, and it was the best party I ever had. I'm just glad this party wasn't at my house, so I don't have to clean up the mess. And Freddy's cake was so funny."

"You liked the party?" I asked.

"Oh, yes," Mrs. Hendricks said. She told Chief Glendale, "I can give them a good reference."

We had done it. The aliens had thrown a magnificent Alien Party.

Mom told Chief Glendale, "Sure, we can help with the parade."

Dad put his arm around Mom's shoulder and pulled her close.  "Yes, a parade should be as easy as flying from star to star."

I groaned. Now I needed a Parade List.

Mrs. Hendricks laughed. "You need to start a company. I can help you with the legal papers. What will you call your company?"

I knew the answer to that one. "Aliens, Inc."

Looking around the alien landscape with the swirling green glow, everyone agreed it was a good name.

Out-of-this-world Events

Now it was time for presents.

Mom and Dad piled everything on a table on the deck.

I stayed close to Mrs. Lynx, though, because she was talking to Chief Glendale.

"Someone in the third grade used telekinesis," she said. "Mr. Smith didn't fall hard enough. From now on, I will be watching the whole third grade."

Chief Glendale patted her on the back. "When you find the aliens, you just let me know."

I didn't know if he believed her or not. But from now on, we had to worry about Mrs. Lynx and Chief Glendale.

Next, Freddy and Bree opened their presents. There were lots of toys, games and books. Last, Bree opened my present, a framed picture of Jupiter.

"Thanks. This is magnificent. But how did you get this picture?" Bree's forehead wrinkled. "It's taken from space."

I was ready for that one. "The space program takes pictures from their space ships. It's easy to find them on the Internet."

"Oh," she said. "For a minute, I thought you took the picture yourself."

Then came the best part of the Alien Party, the tree houses. All the parents and teachers and Mrs. Lynx left. Bree and Mom and the girls climbed up to one spaceship for a sleepover. Freddy and Dad and the guys and I climbed up to the other spaceship for a sleepover, too.

But just as I was climbing up, I sneezed. And suddenly, the itching was really bad.

"Dad, I have to go inside for a while," I whispered in his ear.

Dad nodded. "The worst time for this to happen."

I sprinted up to my bedroom. Sitting on the floor in front of a mirror, I scratched at the top of my head until a piece of skin came off. What a bad time to have to shed my skin, but it would only take an hour to get it off my face and hands. The rest would be covered up with clothes, so no one would see.

I wiggled a finger into the small hole and started stretching and pulling at the skin on my face. I had just loosened a long piece from my forehead to chin when I heard my bedroom door open.

Was it Chief Glendale? Was it Mrs. Lynx?

"What are you doing?" said a voice. "And I want the truth, the whole truth and nothing but the truth."

It was Bree.

So, I told her, "I am shedding my skin."

And Bree said, "Alien boys are weird."

THE END

FOR FUN

THESE BUGS ARE HIDDEN SOMEWHERE WITHIN THE PAGES OF THIS BOOK. CAN YOU FIND ALL OF THEM?

ONE EXTRA BUG IS HIDDEN SOMEWHERE IN THE BOOK, TOO. CAN YOU FIND IT?

The Answers are at MimsHouse.com/aliens

PREVIEW
THE ALIENS, INC. SERIES,
BOOK 2

KELL, and the HORSE APPLE PARADE

By Darcy Pattison

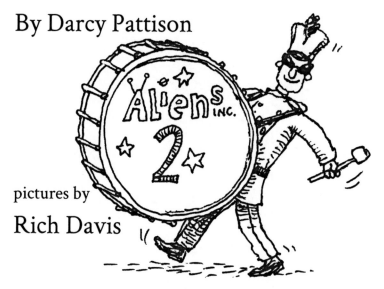

pictures by
Rich Davis

Mims House / Little Rock, AR

CHAPTER

"Kell, we need to plan the Friends of Police parade," Mary Lee Glendale said.

I swiped a streak of red across my paper. I sat at an art table with Mary Lee and my best friend, Bree Hendricks.

Mrs. Crux, the art teacher, had shown us a painting by Alexander Calder called "Red Nose." Now, we were painting red noses.

"Will you march in the parade?" I asked.

"My dad is president of the FOP. That's what we call the Friends of Police, the FOP. I always march in the parade," Mary Lee said. "Will you?"

"No." I rubbed my right eye and stared at the Red Nose on my paper. It was a good thing she didn't ask, "Why?" She just kept talking.

"I think the parade should have superheroes and superheroines," Mary Lee said.

My family runs Aliens, Inc. which plans and puts on parties and other special events. The FOP parade was in one month and this was our first time to plan a parade. We were nervous. Mom and Dad said I couldn't march because too many people would see me. That was dangerous for us.

Bree said, "The best superheroes are aliens."

I glared at Bree for even talking about aliens. She was painting a very long, very skinny red nose. Probably a red elephant nose.

Mary Lee said, "Superheroes aren't aliens."

Bree said, "Superman is from the planet of Krypton. He's an alien."

"My Dad says Krypton was a fantastic planet," I said.

"How would he know?" Mary Lee asked. "You can't really go there."

But she was wrong.

Bree looked up and grinned at me. She saw me peeling the skin off my face last week. I had to tell her the truth, the whole truth and nothing but the truth. I, Kell Smith, am an alien from the planet of Bix. No one else knows except Bree. Well, my parents know, too. And Dad really did go to Krypton before it blew up.

But I can't tell Mary Lee that.

I dipped my brush into black paint. I put a black line around the red nose. I studied the painting. Was this the nose of an elephant? Or the nose of Freddy Rubin? I looked over at Freddy and then back at my painting. I looked at the painting and then at Freddy. Yes, this was Freddy's nose!

He has brown eyes. I raised my hand. "Mrs. Crux, do we have brown paint for the eyes?"

"Yes," she said. "In the cabinet. You may get it."

Mary Lee squinted at me while she asked, "Is there silver paint, too?"

"Yes," Mrs. Crux said.

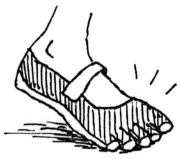

But just then, Principal Lynx came into the room. She wore barefoot shoes, the kind that shows each toe. They were sneaky shoes. She glided around, looking over the shoulders of students. When she does that, it gives me the creeps because she is an alien chaser. I don't want her to catch me.

I decided to wait to get the brown and silver paints.

Mrs. Lynx stopped behind Mary Lee and said, "I am very excited about the FOP parade. It's just the sort of thing to bring out the aliens. They love to see humans making fools of themselves."

Mary Lee cocked an eye at me and then at the principal. "Mrs. Lynx, I don't think aliens will come to the parade. Just people dressed up like super-heroes and superheroines."

"Mark my words," said Mrs. Lynx. "Aliens will be sneaking around the parade. And I will catch them."

I shivered.

Mrs. Lynx turned to me. "Please thank your parents for taking on the FOP parade."

"Yes, ma'am." I said.

Mrs. Edith Bumfrey had planned the FOP parade for the last 23 years. But last month, a rich aunt died and left her a house in Hawaii. After she moved, the FOP hired us. But if Mrs. Lynx planned to stalk aliens at the parade, maybe we shouldn't plan it. Except we needed the money.

Mrs. Lynx took a cell phone from her pocket and clicked on an app. Then she leaned over Bree's painting to see it better. "Is that an alien nose? It looks like an alien nose, and I would know."

"No, ma'am," she said. "It is an anteater nose."

Mrs. Lynx nodded solemnly. "Ah, I see that now."

There are animals that EAT ants? I didn't know that. I hate bugs of any kind. On Earth, there are more bugs than any other kind of creature. You can never tell which bugs will bite. Or sting. I made a decision: I wanted an anteater for a pet.

Just then, Mrs. Lynx's phone jingled with piano music. Her mouth made a circle, like she was trying to say the word, "Oh." Quick, she looked up and stared at Bree. She frowned and looked at the phone again and shook it.

Mrs. Crux patted Mrs. Lynx's shoulder and said, "Did you get it?"

The principal's face lit up with a big smile. "Yes. Want to see?"

When Mrs. Crux nodded, they went over to the supply cabinet and turned their backs to the class. I had to know what they were doing.

I walked to the supply cabinet and did a thing called eavesdropping. Eaves are part of a house's roof. This doesn't make sense to me. Eaves-dropping means that you listen to someone talking when they don't want you to listen. Did humans hang from rooftops and listen to other people talking?

Mrs. Lynx was saying, "—best app for finding an alien."

"Fantastic. How much did it cost?" asked Mrs. Crux.

"A fortune. But I

am the President of S.A.C., the Society of Alien Chasers. So, I got a discount. But this app didn't come cheap."

My mouth made an "Oh." I shivered. How was I going to keep away from Mrs. Lynx and her app? "What does it do when you find an alien?" asked Mrs. Crux.

Mrs. Lynx laughed. "Here's the good part. It just sounds like a ring tone. But aliens are smart. You can't just use an alien sound or alien music. Instead, it plays a cowboy song."

"I am from Australia, mate," Mrs. Crux said. "I don't know any American cowboy songs."

"Does Australia even have aliens?" Mrs. Lynx asked. "The app plays 'Home on the Range.'"

I had heard enough. I grabbed a jar of brown paint and turned to go. But I was so nervous that I slammed the cabinet door.

Mrs. Lynx whirled around and squinted at me. "Wait. Were you listening?"

My eyes got big and my hands shook. The bottle of brown paint dropped. Splat!

Brown paint splattered all over my tennis shoes.

And all over Mrs. Crux's tennis shoes.

Even Mrs. Lynx's barefoot shoes were wet with brown splotches.

"Oh, I am sorry," I cried.

Mrs. Crux shook her head at me and smiled, "No worries, mate. It's just another Accidental Art. Aja, bring us some of that paper." She pointed to large white sheets of paper.

Mrs. Crux and Mrs. Lynx and I walked all over the paper. I stayed behind Mrs. Lynx and made sure her phone never pointed at me. We made brown barefoot shoe prints and tennis shoe prints and smears. We thumbtacked the picture to the Accidental

Art bulletin board. That made eleven Accidental Arts for me. But it was the first Accidental Art for Mrs. Crux and the first for Mrs. Lynx.

After that, they went to the teacher's lounge to wash up their shoes. I washed my shoes at the sink in the art room.

"Ouch!"

I spun around to see who said that. Mary Lee stood by the supply cabinet shaking her hand and arm. "Something bit me."

Bree and Aja Dalal rushed over to Mary Lee.

"What happened?" Bree said.

"What do you mean, 'something bit you'?" Aja said.

"There!" Mary Lee pointed.

"That's nothing," Aja said. "Just a small brown spider. Hey, Kell," he called to me, "did you spill brown paint on this spider?"

"Ha, ha," I said, "Very funny."

Aja took off his shoe and slammed it against the cabinet. "It's dead now."

I was not going close to that cabinet again. Because I do not like spiders, especially biting spiders.

Just then, the bell rang and it was time to go to the next class.

On the way out, Mary Lee said, "You forgot to bring me the silver paint."

"Why did you need silver?"

"I wanted to paint an alien boy with a red nose and silver eyes," she said. Then, she slapped my shoulder and left.

Wait. How does an Earth girl know that alien boys have silver eyes?

READ MORE ADVENTURES WITH KELL, BREE AND THE ALIENS, INC. GANG IN BOOK 2:

KELL AND THE HORSE APPLE PARADE

Join our mailing list.

MimsHouse.com/newsletter/

Other Books in
The Aliens, Inc. Series

Book 2: *Kell and the Horse Apple Parade (2014)*
Book 3: *Kell and the Giants (2014)*
Book 4: *Kell and the Detectives (2015)*

Other Books by Darcy Pattison

Saucy and Bubba: A Hansel and Gretel Tale

The Girl, the Gypsy and the Gargyole

Vagabonds

Abayomi, the Brazilian Puma:

Wisdom, the Midway Albatross:

The Scary Slopes

Prairie Storms

Desert Baths

19 Girls and Me

Searching for Oliver K. Woodman

The Journey of Oliver K. Woodman

The River Dragon

ABOUT THE AUTHOR & ILLUSTRATOR

Translated into eight languages, children's book author **DARCY PATTISON** writes picture books, middle grade novels, and children's nonfiction. Previous titles include *The Journey of Oliver K. Woodman* (Harcourt), *Searching for Oliver K. Woodman* (Harcourt), *The Wayfinder* (Greenwillow), *19 Girls and Me* (Philomel), *Prairie Storms* (Sylvan Dell), *Desert Baths* (Desert Baths), and *Wisdom, the Midway Albatross* (Mims House.) Her work has been recognized by **starred reviews** in *Kirkus, BCCB,* and *PW. Desert Baths* was named a 2013 Outstanding Science Trade Book and the *Library Media Connection,* Editor's Choice. She is a member of the Society of Children's Bookwriters and Illustrators and the Author's Guild. For more information, see darcypattison.com.

RICH DAVIS, illustrator for the Aliens, Inc series has wondered, "What could be better than getting to do black and white cartoon work for a sci-fi easy reader?" Working on this book has been one big fun-making experience. Rich has also illustrated 12 other children's books, including beginning reader series, *Tiny the Big Dog* (Penguin). His joy is to help kids develop creatively and he has invented a simple drawing game (Pick and Draw.com) and an activities book as a fun tool that now have a following around the world. He frequently does programs at schools and libraries in order to draw with thousands of kids yearly. For him, it is a dream come true and he recognizes that the source is from God alone.

CPSIA information can be obtained at www.ICGtesting.com
Printed in the USA
LVOW08s1556300914

406573LV00016B/900/P